*T*his Puffin book belongs to

_____

Anything
for You

PUFFIN BOOKS

Published by the Penguin Group
Penguin Books Ltd, 80 Strand, London WC2R 0RL, England
Penguin Group (USA), Inc., 375 Hudson Street, New York, New York 10014, USA
Penguin Books Australia Ltd, 250 Camberwell Road, Camberwell, Victoria 3124, Australia
Penguin Books Canada Ltd, 10 Alcorn Avenue, Toronto, Ontario, Canada M4V 3B2
Penguin Books India (P) Ltd, 11 Community Centre, Panchsheel Park, New Delhi – 110 017, India
Penguin Books (NZ) Ltd, Cnr Rosedale and Airborne Roads, Albany, Auckland, New Zealand
Penguin Books (South Africa) (Pty) Ltd, 24 Sturdee Avenue, Rosebank 2196, South Africa

Penguin Books Ltd, Registered Offices: 80 Strand, London WC2R 0RL, England

www.penguin.com

First published 2003
First published in paperback 2004
1 3 5 7 9 10 8 6 4 2

Text copyright © John Wallace, 2003
Illustrations copyright © Harry Horse, 2003
All rights reserved

The moral right of the author and illustrator has been asserted

Set in Sabon

Made and printed in China

British Library Cataloguing in Publication Data
A CIP catalogue record for this book is available from the British Library

ISBN 0–140–56926–X

Anything for You

JOHN WALLACE

Illustrated by HARRY HORSE

PUFFIN

For William, Sammy and Isaac – JW

For Derek – HH

It was nearly bedtime at the end of a very long day.

Little Charlie had been trying to help Ginger,

but somehow things kept going wrong.

Little Charlie
had tried to help
Ginger by
cleaning up
the garden.

He'd done some digging . . .

. . . and collected some apples . . .

. . . but all he made was a mess.

So Little Charlie tried even harder to help
Ginger by cleaning up the house.

But all he made was an even *bigger* mess.

"Oh dear!" said Ginger.
"Instead of cleaning the house up,
we need to clean you up!"

Ginger ran a bath for Little Charlie.
"Could you get in, please?"
asked Ginger.

"Right away!"
replied Little Charlie.
"I'd do

anything
   for you."

"I'd swim to the end of the bath for you!"
said Little Charlie.

"And all the way back again!"

"Would you?" said Ginger, as he lifted
Little Charlie out of the bath.

"Let's get you dry, shall we?"

"I'd climb to the top
of a really tall
tree for you!"
said Little
Charlie.

"Would
you?"
said
Ginger.

"I'd smile
my biggest smile
for you," said
Little Charlie.

"*And* draw
a special picture
for you . . .

. . . *and* give you all
my money!"

"Ginger," whispered Little Charlie,
"I'd even let you be my
best friend."

"You would?" replied Ginger.

"I would!" said Little Charlie.

"Because I'd do

anything for you."

"Anything?"
asked Ginger.

"Anything," replied Little Charlie.

Then Ginger had an idea.

It had been such a long day and he saw

that Little Charlie was looking very tired.

"So you'd do **anything for me,**" Ginger said, as he thought for a moment.

"Would you get into bed for me?" he asked.

"Anything,"

said Little Charlie proudly.

"Would you snuggle down for me?"
asked Ginger, gently tucking Little Charlie in.

"Anything," said Little Charlie,
snuggling down deeply.

"Would you shut your eyes for me?"
asked Ginger, more quietly this time.

"Anything,"
yawned
Little Charlie.

"Would you sleep tight for me?"
whispered Ginger.

"Anything . . ."
murmured Little Charlie.

"Would you sleep tight, all night
long, for me?" whispered Ginger.

But Little Charlie said nothing,

because he was already fast asleep.

Ginger gave him a goodnight kiss.

"And I'd do **anything for you** too,"
said Ginger.

"Sleep well, my little one."